Eat Me Kindly

By Andi Katsina

Vol 1 : Oranges

11218
10

Published by The Indie Oracle

ISBN; 978- 0-955579516

www.theindieoracle.com

First Edition

Dedicated to ;

My Good Friend

Sally Gamble.

My name is Olho Jupitar.

Along, long time ago
I lived on a tiny asteroid
with the rest of my family.

One day a spaceship flew by so fast,

it sent us off course.

Fortunately there was a planet close by. We safely landed on Earth.

When we were falling
through your atmosphere,
bright orange fire surrounded us.

This is what we used to look like

when we first landed on Earth

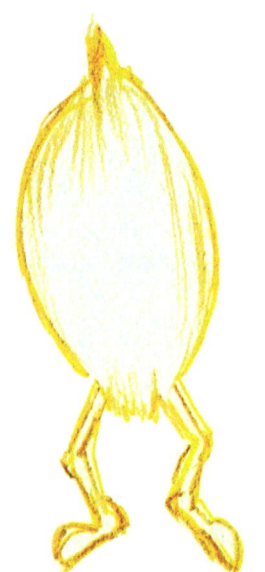  

Some of your people call us pips,
Some of your people call us seeds.

The horrible Iklant Gulls that lived on your planet in the dinosaur era, used to swoop down from the sky

whenever they saw us,

and gobble us up.

One day a summit meeting was held to find a way to stop the gulls eating my kind.

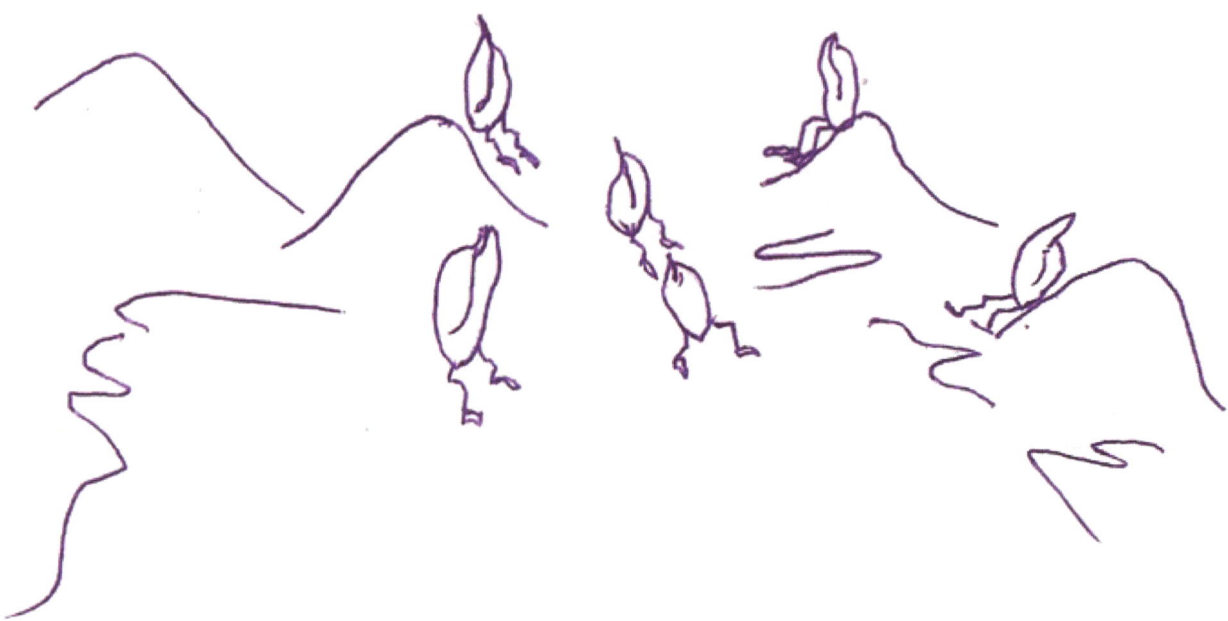

Remembering the bright fiery glow we saw when
we came to your planet, and knowing that
the Iklant Gulls were afraid of fire,
we believed that if we could camouflage
ourselves to look like fire, the gulls

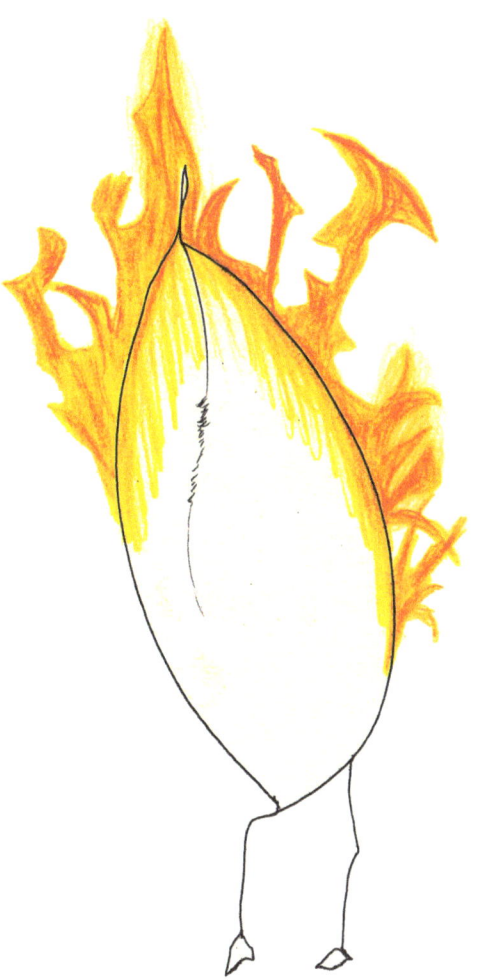

would stop hunting us.

There were so many ideas. Finally a decision was made. This was the design we chose:

We called it a fireball suit.

We designed a suit that would keep us safe
and at the same time nourish us,
and provide lots of energy.

We built a thick, but pliable outside wall, called an exocarp.

Inside we designed

small carpels for us to live in.

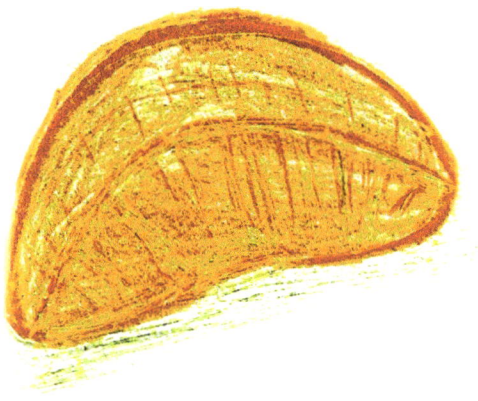

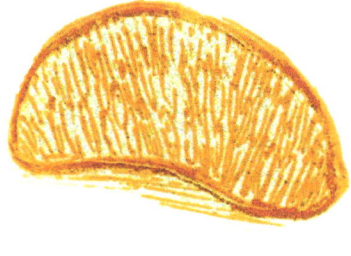

These are carpels

We made the carpels broad on the outside, narrowing towards the inner edge. We did this so that when a group of them were slotted together, they formed an oval shape:

The fireball was a beautiful,

warm bright fire colour.

When we began living inside the fireball suits, the Iklant Gulls, still trying to swoop down and attack us,

seeing the bright fire colour of our new home,

quickly flew away, screaming, 'orhrannge, orhrannge'. It was the first time we'd ever known

the gulls to be afraid.

The gulls thought our new dwellings

were little balls of fire.

After the Iklant Gulls, and all the dinosaurs, disappeared, your people stopped living in caves, and began taking care of our fireball suits.

They gave us lots of water, and
built beautiful green trees with white flowers,
so that we could bathe in the sunshine,
and feel the gentle splash of rain, when it fell.

Because your ancestors looked after us and gave us trees to hang from, now, every year, we like to be picked from the tree, giving us a chance to change our fireball suit.

Please eat lots of the carpels found inside the fireballs. This way you release us from our fireball suits.

Also, as a gift, we give to you,
all of our special powers and goodness
locked inside the fireball carpels.

When you eat the carpels, all the nourishment contained within the orange fireballs will flow into you, making you feel strong and happy. They will help to always keep you healthy.

Eat Me Kindly

Fireballs are chocked full of energy, vitamins, minerals, health, happy!

Here are some fun ways you can enjoy them. Fireballs are easy to carry, so you can take them with you, to eat, anywhere.

Peel the fireball... [Eat Me]

Separate the carpels... [Eat Me]

You can slice the fireball into thin wafers... [Eat Me]

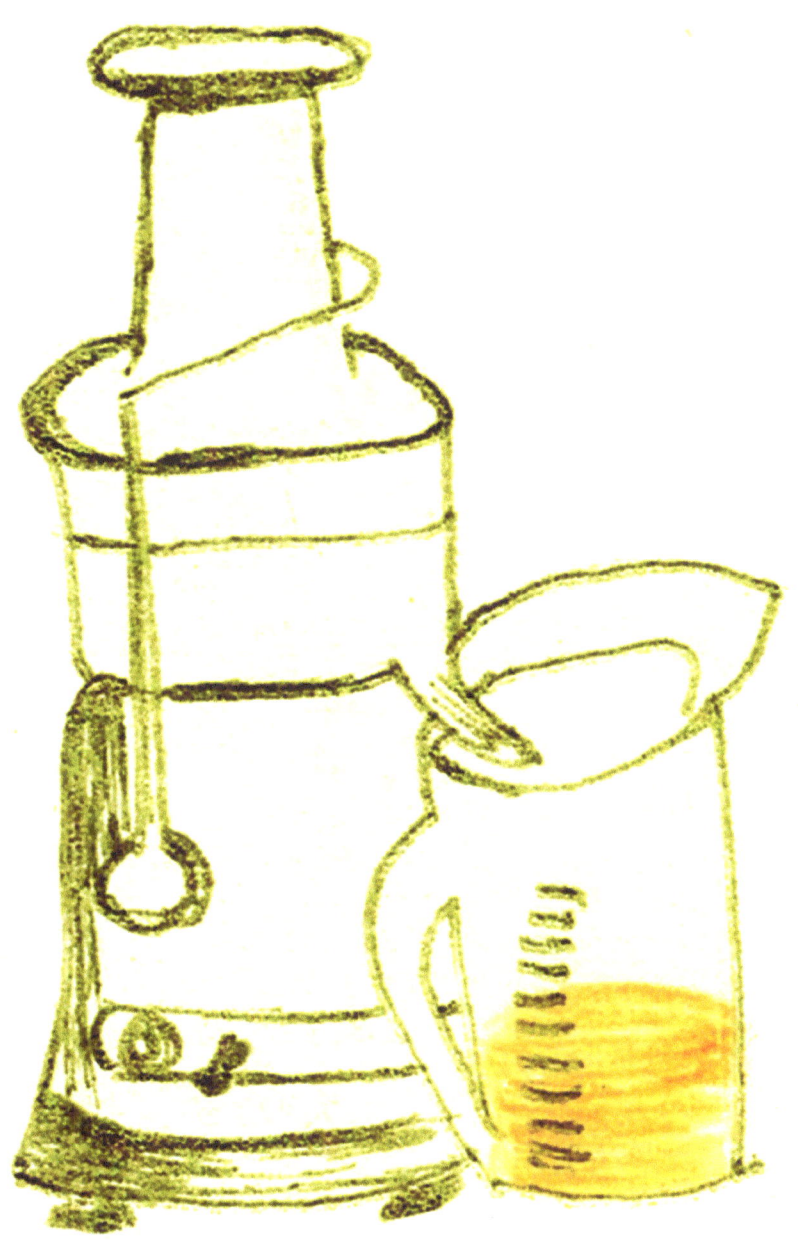

Put carpels into a juice extractor, to
make fresh & delicious juice...[Eat Me]

By adding small pieces of the fireball carpels

to other pieces of fruit,

you can make a tasty fruit-salad... [Eat Me]

It is easy to make marmalade using the fireball suit... [Eat Me]

To make a spicy taste,
you can sprinkle a little
masala or chilli powder
on the carpels.

This gives them a different flavour, but they are still super juicy... [Eat Me]

The only thing I ask of you is this;

when enjoying the carpels found inside an orange fireball, if you come across any pips or seeds sleeping in the fireball, please don't swallow them, or wake them up.

Simply throw
them away in the usual manner,
but first shake them in your hand and whisper;
1, 2, 3 please be free.

This way they will eventually find
their way back to a fireball tree.

Please accept our gift, to you. I call them fireballs

some of my family call them Orhrannges in honour of the fact that they allowed us to live in your world

by protecting us from the Iklant Gulls.

Remember that originally we came from

far, far away,

and have many special powers.

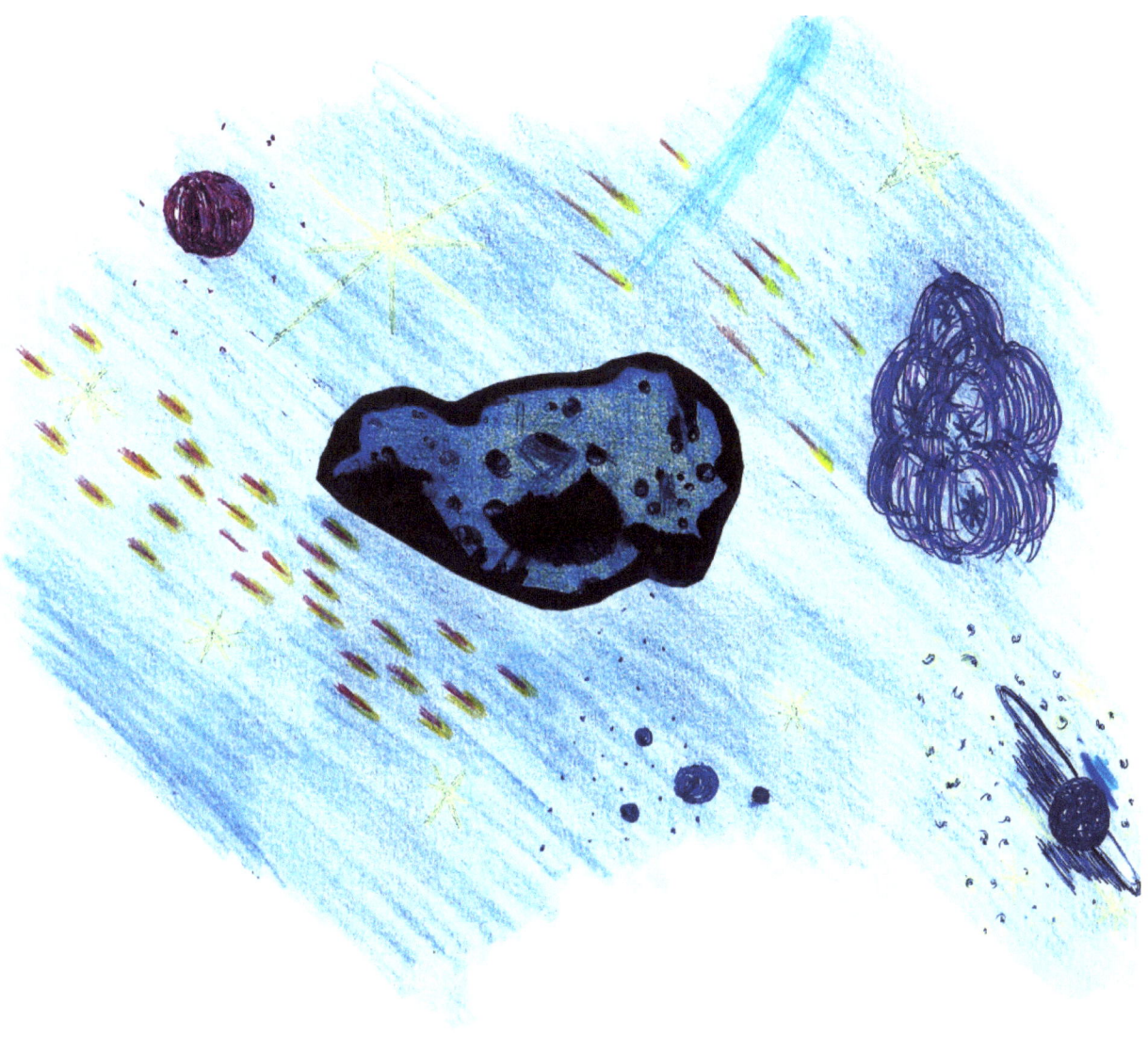

If you eat our fireballs, often,

you will feel these special powers too.

They will flow throughout your body

helping you to always feel

healthy & happy!

Want to know more about our fireball suits?
Check out the Bio I prepared for you.

FIREBALLS Botanical Info	
Other Names	Orhrannge, Orange
Kingdom	Plantae
Division	Mangoliophyta
Order	Sapindales
Family	Rutaceae
Genus	Citrus
Species	Citrus Sinensis
Hang on Tree	Evergreens
Flowers on Tree	White
Leaves on Tree	Green

FIREBALLS Nutritional Info	
NUTRIMENTS	
Antioxidants	High
Vitamin C	High
Minerals	Rich
Vitamins	Rich

Fireballs and the carpels inside, are fantastic for the growth & development of all human children.

When we know you are eating our fireballs,

we are very happy

Write down why you like to eat oranges:

Name..

Age..

City...

Country..

Favourite game..

I like orange fireballs because

_____

_____

_____

_____

_____

_____

_____

_____

_____

_____

_____

_____

*Signed by*_____

Other books in the Eat Me Kindly Series

VOLUMES

35	Pineapple
36	Kale
37	Passion Fruit
38	Asparagus
39	Pak Choy
40	Coconut

Thank you for reading about Olho Jupitar

Other books by Andi Katsina

Gurk & Whale
[The Rose Mane Arrows]
By Andi Katsina
ISBN; 978-0-9555795-0-9

•♥*•*

From the Rick & Wylie's Fantastical Magical Adventures trilogy;

Rick & Wylie's Fantastical, Magical Adventures   *Book 1*
[Journey to the Kingdom]
By Andi Katsina
ISBN; 978-0-9555795-2-3

Rick & Wylie's Fantastical, Magical Adventures   *Book 2*
[Hot Pursuit on the Road to Discovery]
By Andi Katsina
ISBN; 978-0-9555795-5-4

•♥*•*

www.ingramcontent.com/pod-product-compliance
Lightning Source LLC
Chambersburg PA
CBHW041012170626
46815CB00003B/269